Willie Wins

written by Almira Astudillo Gilles

illustrated by Carl Angel

Lee & Low Books Inc.
New York

LEE & LOW BOOKS Inc., 95 Madison Avenue, New York, NY 10016
leeandlow.com

Manufactured in China by South China Printing Co.

Book design by Cathleen O'Brien
Book production by The Kids at Our House

The text is set in Novarese
The illustrations are rendered in acrylic

The artist would like to thank Lakeview Elementary School; and Martin, Abe,
Tony, Eddie, Laura, Amy, Mickey, Christina, and Barry for posing as models for
the characters in this book.

HC 10 9 8 7 6 5 4 3
PB 10 9 8 7 6 5 4 3 2 1
First Edition

Library of Congress Cataloging-in-Publication Data
Gilles, Almira Astudillo.
Willie wins / by Almira Astudillo Gilles ; illustrated by Carl Angel.—1st ed.
p.   cm.
Summary: Willie's father tells him there is something special in an old coconut bank
brought from the Philippines, but Willie is embarrassed to take it to school for a
contest, especially since he knows that one of his classmates will make fun of him.
ISBN-13: 978-1-58430-023-6 (hc)   ISBN-13: 978-1-60060-237-5 (pb)
[1. Fathers and sons—Fiction. 2. Filipino Americans—Fiction. 3. Schools—Fiction.]
I. Angel, Carl, ill. II. Title.
PZ7.G4025Wi2001   [Fic]—dc21   00-061934

For Isabel and Matthew, who have taught me to look
for treasure in unlikely places —A.A.G.

To Richard, Sarah, Kelsey, Emma, and Sophia —C.A.

"I can't believe you struck out in the last inning!" Stan snarled at Willie.

Willie felt his face burning as he bent to pick up his baseball glove. He turned away and trudged over to Dad.

"Here comes my favorite baseball player," Dad said, ruffling Willie's hair. "You know, we didn't have Little League when I was a boy. My friends and I played on the street with bamboo bats and a rolled-up sock."

Willie sighed. He didn't want to hear any of Dad's stories from the Philippines. He just couldn't get Stan out of his mind.

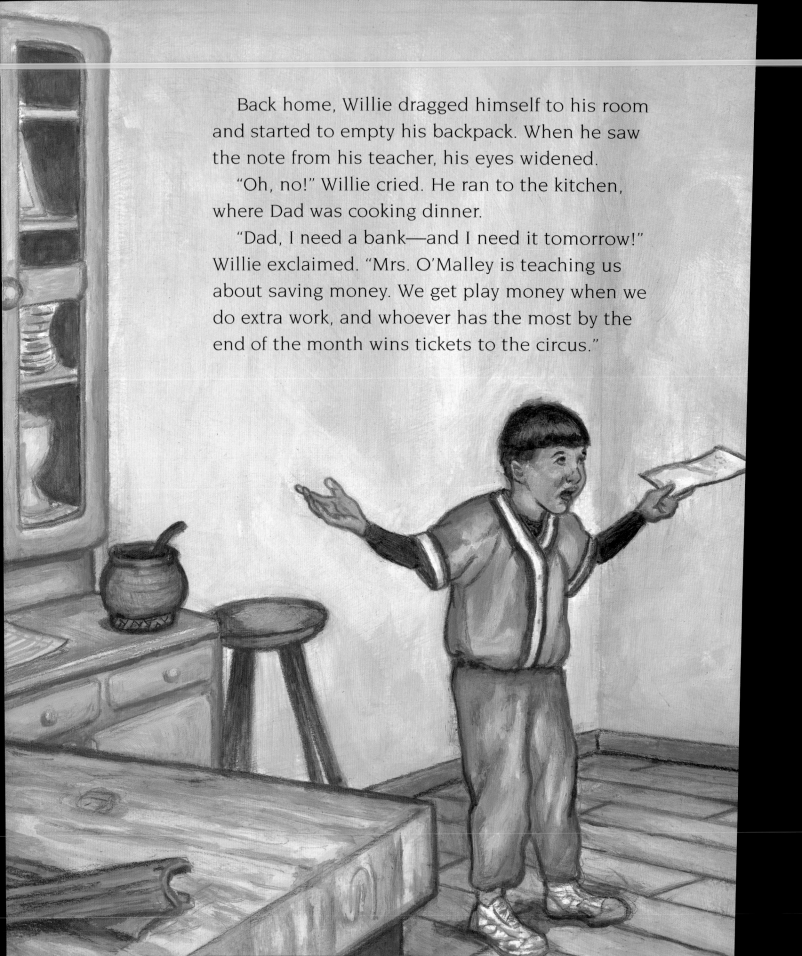

Back home, Willie dragged himself to his room and started to empty his backpack. When he saw the note from his teacher, his eyes widened.

"Oh, no!" Willie cried. He ran to the kitchen, where Dad was cooking dinner.

"Dad, I need a bank—and I need it tomorrow!" Willie exclaimed. "Mrs. O'Malley is teaching us about saving money. We get play money when we do extra work, and whoever has the most by the end of the month wins tickets to the circus."

Dad rubbed his chin, thinking. Then he smiled. "I've got just the thing," he said. "I was saving it for your birthday, but now seems like the perfect time."

Willie followed Dad to the basement and watched him dig out a rusty metal box.

"Open it," Dad said, his eyes twinkling.

Inside, Willie found a wooden ball with a slit as long as the palm of his hand.

"What is it?" Willie asked.

"It's an alkansiya," Dad said proudly. "It used to be the shell of a coconut. Now it's a bank."

Willie frowned. "But Dad, I just need a regular bank, like a pig or a car."

He turned the coconut bank over and noticed a tiny hole. "What's this for?"

"That's for the ants," Dad explained. "They crawl in, and after they've eaten all the coconut meat they crawl out. Then the shell is scrubbed and polished."

Willie liked the idea of ants marching through the hole, gobbling up the meat, and then marching out again. But he still wasn't sure about the bank.

"You have to crack this open to get the money out," Willie said. "After that, you can't use it anymore."

"Ah," said Dad. "That's why it's such a great bank. It's sneak-proof!"

"Plus, there's something special inside this alkansiya," Dad added more seriously.

"When I was your age my uncle gave me a present when he visited from San Francisco. It was the only thing I ever got from the States, so I guarded it like a treasure. Years later, when I moved here, I put the treasure in my alkansiya. I wanted to save it for my own child."

He patted Willie on the back. "I guess that's you."

Willie shook the bank. He thought he heard a soft rustle. "What is it?" he asked.

Dad winked. "You'll know in a month."

Willie sighed. It was such a strange-looking bank. But what if Dad was right and there was something special inside?

The next day, Willie watched as his classmates pulled out their banks. Three kids had piggy banks, Sally had a silver train, and Alonzo had a gumball machine with real candy.

My bank sure is different, Willie thought as he slowly lifted the alkansiya out of the box.

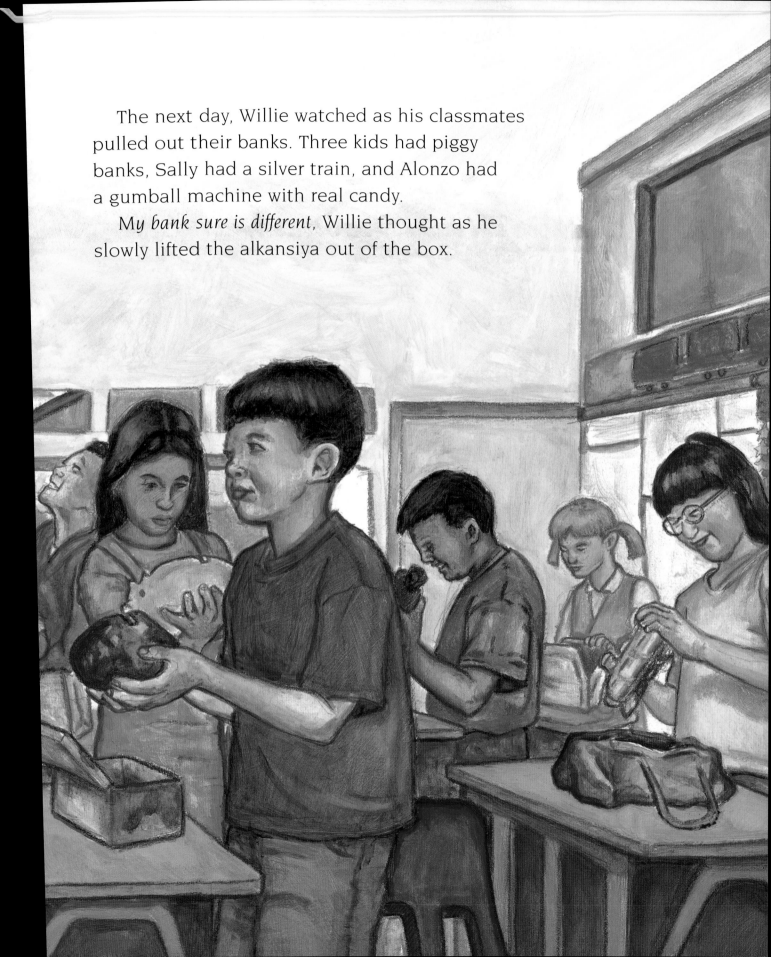

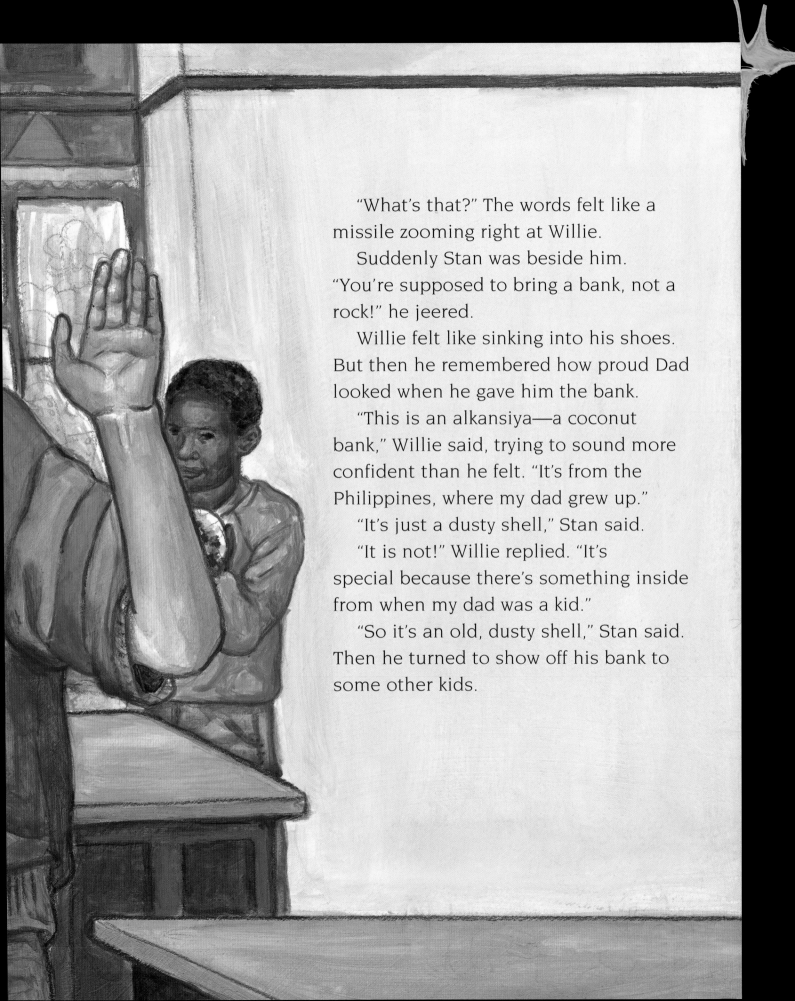

"What's that?" The words felt like a missile zooming right at Willie.

Suddenly Stan was beside him. "You're supposed to bring a bank, not a rock!" he jeered.

Willie felt like sinking into his shoes. But then he remembered how proud Dad looked when he gave him the bank.

"This is an alkansiya—a coconut bank," Willie said, trying to sound more confident than he felt. "It's from the Philippines, where my dad grew up."

"It's just a dusty shell," Stan said.

"It is not!" Willie replied. "It's special because there's something inside from when my dad was a kid."

"So it's an old, dusty shell," Stan said. Then he turned to show off his bank to some other kids.

Willie looked down, blinking hard. Then he felt a hand on his shoulder.

"Just ignore Stan," said Matt, Willie's best friend. "He's still mad because he thinks you made the team lose yesterday."

Matt looked curiously at Willie's bank. "I've never seen anything like this," he said. "What do you think's inside? It must be something really special."

Willie nodded slowly, only half-believing.

Stan turned back to Willie and pointed at the alkansiya. "That's a loser's bank," he taunted. "It's ugly, and I'll bet it's empty, too."

That did it. Willie stepped up to Stan. "My dad is no liar! If he says there's something special inside, then there must be something special."

"We'll see," Stan snickered.

Willie stood up tall and made himself a promise. By the end of the month his bank would be full of money *and* the treasure.

For the next four weeks, Willie worked so hard that he barely had time to play with Matt after school.

One evening, Dad came to Willie's room for a game of catch. "Need a break, son?" he asked.

Willie shook his head. "Not now, Dad. I'm too busy."

"Some other time, then," Dad answered. "Don't worry. With all the work you're doing, I'm sure you'll do great."

Stan was working hard too, and he picked on Willie almost every day. Willie tried to be as tough as his coconut bank, but he was still worried. What if Stan was making more money? And what if Dad's treasure wasn't really a treasure, but something only Dad thought was special, like the wooden water buffalo he kept on his desk?

Finally, the end of the month arrived. "It's time to unlock your banks," Mrs. O'Malley announced.

Click-click-click! Keys were inserted into locks, lids flipped open, and play money dumped on desks. There were whoops and shrieks of excitement.

Willie sat through it all, his heart thumping. The small hammer Dad had given him felt so heavy.

Mrs. O'Malley walked over to Willie. "Go ahead," she urged him gently.

Willie took a deep breath. Then he whacked the bank with one sure stroke like Dad had told him. Play money whirled all over his desk and onto the floor. No one made a sound.

Then Mrs. O'Malley looked at her notebook. "You all worked really hard," she said to the class, "but according to my official tally, Willie is the winner."

Stan stood with his arms crossed. "Well, where's the treasure?" he demanded.

Willie looked among the jagged pieces of the broken bank. He sifted through the money on his desk. Nothing. A lump formed in his throat. Willie had no idea what he was looking for.

Then he spied a flash of color beside his foot. He bent down and picked up a small card. It had a picture of a brown-skinned man wearing a baseball cap.

"Giants," Willie read from the top of the card.

Stan crouched down beside Willie. "Hey, it's a baseball card!" Stan exclaimed.

As Willie stood up, his classmates crowded around him.

"A San Francisco Giants card!" Matt shouted. "It's WILLIE MAYS, and it's from 1964!"

"Wow," said Stan. "He's one of the greatest baseball players ever! He's in the Hall of Fame! A card that old is probably worth a hundred dollars!"

Willie looked down at the card in his hand.
Dad had come through after all. And he knew Dad
would be waiting proudly when his two favorite
baseball players came home after school.

"Willie," he said, grinning from ear to ear.
"That's me!"